Read it's good! 🙂

PIRATES of the CARIBBEAN

ON STRANGER TIDES

THE VISUAL GUIDE

FOREWORD
by Jerry Bruckheimer

Sometimes you just can't get enough of a good thing. I'd like to think that the main reason we decided to set sail back into the world of Pirates of the Caribbean for a fourth adventure is the same that we kept hearing over and over again from audiences: we missed it! You know, it's like going to camp when you're a kid. You make all these great friends, and then everybody disappears. But now we're all back together again after a break which was just a little too long: Johnny Depp, Geoffrey Rush, Kevin McNally, Keith Richards, screenwriters Ted Elliott and Terry Rossio, cinematographer Dariusz Wolski, costume designer Penny Rose, composer Hans Zimmer, and more. But like any new summer camp session, there are newbies who we're so excited to have join the company, especially director Rob Marshall, actors Penélope Cruz, Ian McShane, Sam Claflin and Astrid Bergés-Frisbey, and production designer John Myhre.

The idea was to take the Pirates of the Caribbean world a few steps beyond, with our new characters engaged in a thrilling and sometimes hilarious search for the fabled Fountain of Youth that takes them from the teeming streets of mid-18th century London to mysterious and dangerous ships and islands inhabited by zombies and mermaids. Stranger tides indeed, all shot in Disney Digital 3-D to make the excitement literally jump off the screen. Our filming began in the jungles, beaches, and oceans of Kauai and Oahu, Hawaii; magnificent environments built in Hollywood; then to a real desert island in Puerto Rico; and finally to historical landmarks and huge studio sets in England. The pages that follow in this book will give you a guided tour through this incredibly visual world that we created for *Pirates of the Caribbean: On Stranger Tides*, and we hope you enjoy the journey both in print, and on screen.

Contents

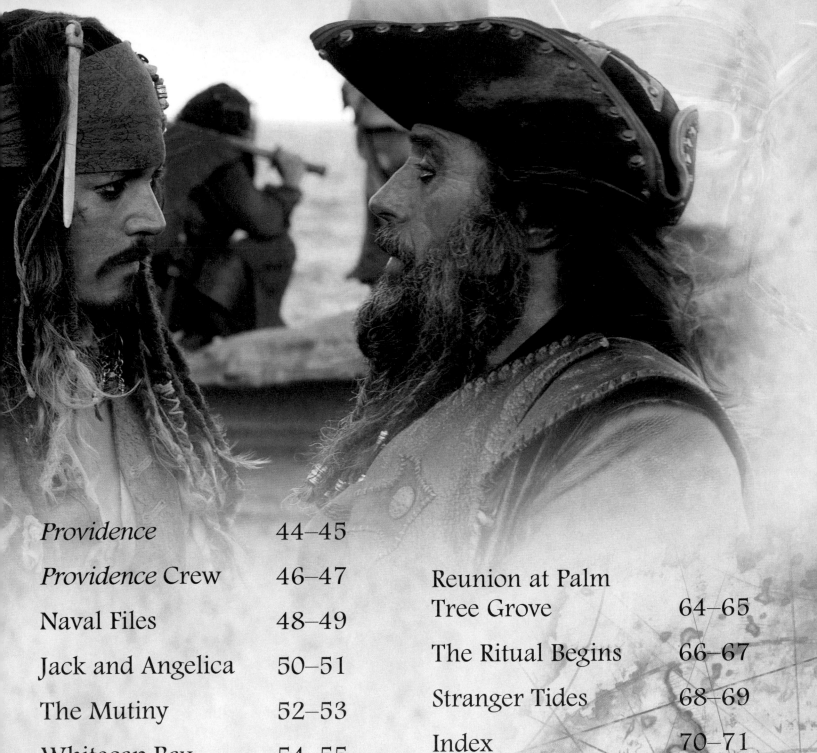

Introduction

Adventure is in the air, savvy? And where there's peril and perfidy you will always find Captain Jack Sparrow—whether he planned it that way or not. The streets of London hide countless secrets, and a fiendish scheme is being hatched to set Jack out on his strangest quest ever—in search of the Fountain of Youth. There's a meeting with, and escape from, a King, and an encounter with the most feared pirate of them all—Blackbeard. Jack will face an old rival and meet a dangerous and mysterious Spanish lady.

Tempted to come aboard? The perils will be many—but there will never be a dull moment!

Having lost his beloved ship, the Black Pearl, Jack is without a ship for any further adventures. And yet, rumors abound that Jack has come to London to recruit a crew...

Captain Jack Sparrow

Each braid and bead in Jack's locks is a souvenir of a different escapade.

Infamous pirate, brigand, highwayman… that's how Jack describes himself. Sailing a fine line between piratical genius and mercurial madness, he has an enemy in every port. Once more, Jack is at the center of intrigue, as he is one of the few mortals to know the location of the Fountain of Youth…

Court in the Act

Far from dreading a court appearance, sly Jack turns up disguised as the judge of his own case. Jack sentences himself to life—but naturally has an escape plan.

Pirate Gear

Jack wears a ragbag of garb from the four corners of the earth. Whether it's a silk headscarf from Singapore or a pistol belt from Port Royal—he hasn't paid for any of it.

True Course

Jack's compass gives him a special edge—as it points to your heart's desire, rather than mere magnetic north. It once belonged to the mystic Tia Dalma.

Wristguard to block enemy blade and to stop blood from dripping onto the handgrip.

Leather sheath protects the sword's blade.

Dress-style tailored linen shirt.

Balancing Act

Even on dry land, a pirate never loses the art of improvization. Trying to stay upright on stormy seas makes a pirate no stranger to keeping his balance in tricky situations.

Key Facts

- Jack begins his new adventure without a ship or crew.

- He is the only man ever to have sentenced himself.

- The way to the Fountain of Youth is committed to his memory.

- He will do anything to regain the Black Pearl.

Pistol inlaid with Spanish silver in elegant floral design.

Hot Shot

Although armed to his gold teeth, Jack rarely needs more than his wits to gain his sly ends.

Did you know?

The quest for the Fountain of Youth began several years back after a pirate showdown with the East India Company. Barbossa stole Jack's ship, the Black Pearl, but Jack found his own small vessel and had already stolen Barbossa's map and set off toward the fountain.

Joshamee Gibbs

Every captain needs a reliable first mate, and Gibbs is Jack Sparrow's first choice. Practical, down-to-earth, and occasionally sensible, Gibbs is everything that Jack is not. They make a great team, but they do have a habit of getting each other into terrible trouble.

Scallywag

This affable ne'er-do-well does have some faults—he is prone to rum-drinking and idleness. He has even been found sleeping in a pigpen.

Gibbs has a rudd' complexion from life on deck.

Did you know?

Gibbs's gray cells hold the most priceless information in the world—the location of the Fountain of Youth. Despite destroying Jack's map, Gibbs keeps its details locked in his memory.

Trusty Flask

Gibbs's flask once contained rum, but if Gibbs is to become part of the Royal Navy, he will have to switch to water.

Leather drinking flask.

Sheathless leather belt with iron buckle.

On Trial

No real resemblance of Captain Jack is in circulation, so his longtime ally Gibbs is tried in a cruel case of mistaken identity. The attitude of the court in London is to hang first and ask questions later—if ever.

Clamshell-style hilt.

Leather swordbelt probably plundered from a previous adventure.

Battle Gear

Humble Joshamee has no truck with newfangled or fancy weapons. He has a cutlass and keeps an antique pistol for sentimental reasons.

Steel trigger guard.

No Escape

When Captain Jack escapes the royal guard, Barbossa threatens to hang Gibbs unless he joins their search for the Fountain of Youth. Gibbs refuses, but can't escape being forced to join the navy, and its quest.

The Spanish

When an old castaway is caught in a fisherman's nets off the coast of Spain, he is found to be clutching a two-hundred-year-old book. Rushed to the royal palace, the book turns out to be the log of the *Santiago*, a Spanish vessel that vanished two centuries before. It tells of explorer Ponce de León's fabled discovery of the long-lost Fountain of Youth. A perilous adventure ensues.

SPANISH OFFICER

THE SPANIARD

The Spaniard

Unknown by any name other than The Spaniard, this enigmatic figure is the one agent that Spanish King Ferdinand has never known to fail. With dashing good looks, he combines hard-won experience with the arrogance of a natural leader. He believes destiny has placed this quest in his hands, and that it will lead him to success.

The Chalices

In the treasure chests of the wrecked *Santiago*, the Spanish captain lays hold of the most valuable prize in Ponce de León's coffers: the silver Chalices of Cartagena. The ancient logbook has revealed their purpose, and now, in this deadly game, the Spanish force holds all the aces.

SPANISH
CAPTAIN

Blade of hard-
tempered steel.

THE
SPANIARD'S
SWORD

Loyal Crew

The Spaniard is assisted by a loyal crew that follows him not out of fear, but through devotion. They would lay down their lives at his merest word. With absolute trust in their leader, none truly knows his purpose on this voyage into the unknown.

Gold finish
on hilt.

Decorated grip
and pommel.

The Santiago's logbook is
bound with a black
leather strap.

The Spaniard's rapier has a
fleur-patterned cup hilt, which
gives it a traditional elegance.

13

The British

Usually, the King of England and his policy makers would not strike a deal with a common pirate like Jack, but these are exceptional times. Rumor has it that the King of Spain knows the location of the Fountain of Youth, and no king likes to be outdone by a rival royal.

Prime Minister

Prime Minister Henry Pelham is a natural politician who knows how to stay on the right side of the King. He is behind the plan to enlist Jack Sparrow, and knows how to track down an elusive pirate.

HENRY PELHAM

King George

Greedy, extravagant, and more interested in exotic food than foreign policy, King George is not a popular ruler. The quest for the Fountain of Youth appeals to his eccentric nature. He loves gambling, so staking his hopes on a cunning pirate strikes him as a pretty good bet.

KING GEORGE

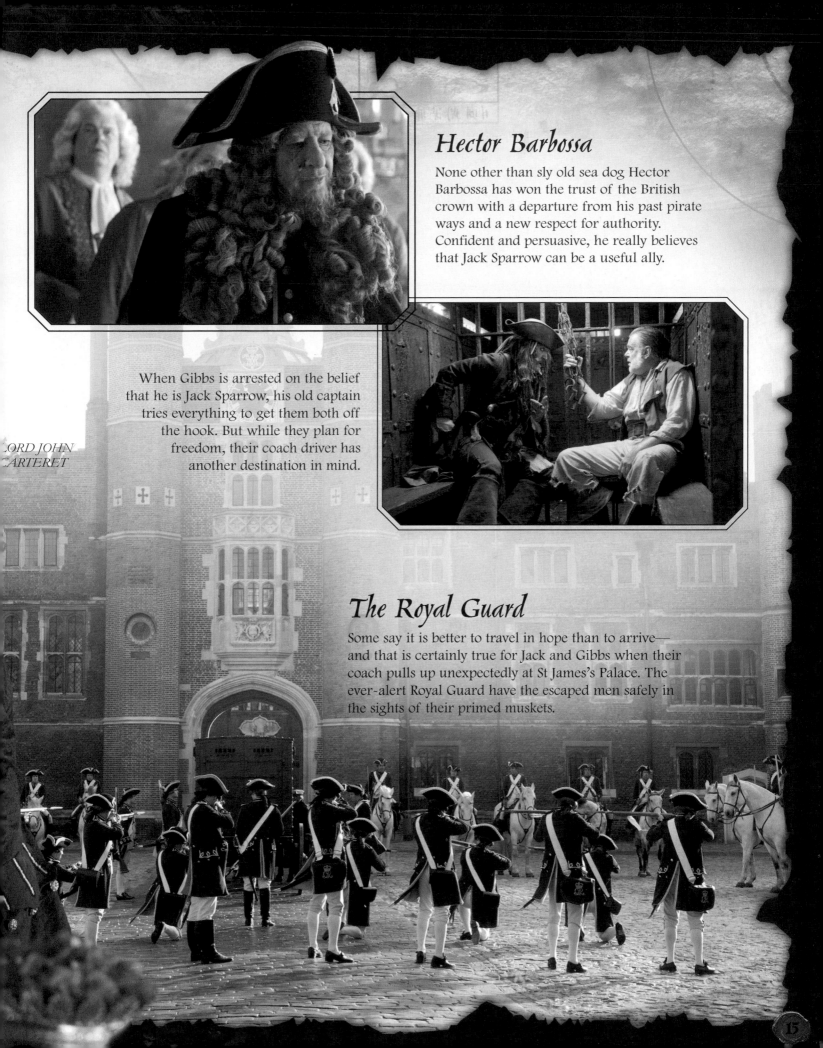

LORD JOHN CARTERET

Hector Barbossa

None other than sly old sea dog Hector Barbossa has won the trust of the British crown with a departure from his past pirate ways and a new respect for authority. Confident and persuasive, he really believes that Jack Sparrow can be a useful ally.

When Gibbs is arrested on the belief that he is Jack Sparrow, his old captain tries everything to get them both off the hook. But while they plan for freedom, their coach driver has another destination in mind.

The Royal Guard

Some say it is better to travel in hope than to arrive—and that is certainly true for Jack and Gibbs when their coach pulls up unexpectedly at St James's Palace. The ever-alert Royal Guard have the escaped men safely in the sights of their primed muskets.

Hector Barbossa

Barbossa always had a high opinion of himself when he was a pirate, but now he is part of the Royal Navy, he is even more self-assured. Yet despite Hector Barbossa's respectable appearance, he has a look in his eye that suggests unsettled scores.

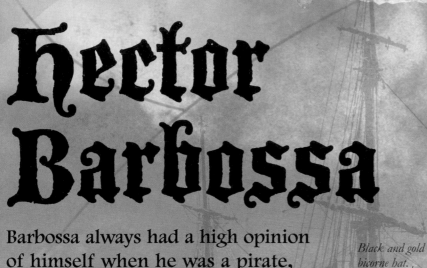

Black and gold bicorne hat.

Pirate Past

Before his change from pirate to privateer, Barbossa cut a flamboyant figure on the high seas. He was extravagantly attired like a celebrity among pirates.

A powdered wig is a sign of high social standing.

A New Man

It seems age and experience have transformed this scurvy sea dog into a respectable pillar of the admiralty. Barbossa is now a hard taskmaster who has forbidden his men from drinking rum and smoking tobacco. As pirates say, there is nothing worse than a reformed person!

Navy blue topcoat with gold brocade.

Flintlock firing mechanism.

Padded underarm rest.

Top Gun

Barbossa has swapped his well-worn pirate's pistol for the best new flintlock design the admiralty arsenal can supply.

Walnut body with brass hardware.

Revenge Trip

The reborn admiral has an old grudge against the infamous pirate Blackbeard. Barbossa's latest mission to find the Fountain of Youth may give him the chance to settle the score once and for all.

Elm shaft.

Lost Items

- The Black Pearl. Barbossa lost his old ship in battle.

- A leg. It was sacrificed in mysterious circumstances.

- His favorite old black hat. Pirates hate to lose their hats.

- His marbles? Barbossa's new hobby is frog-collecting.

Wooden Crutch

One souvenir of Barbossa's life of piracy that will haunt him forever is his recently acquired wooden leg. Fashioned by an admiralty carpenter, his wooden crutch serves its owner well.

Iron-shod foot.

St. James's Palace

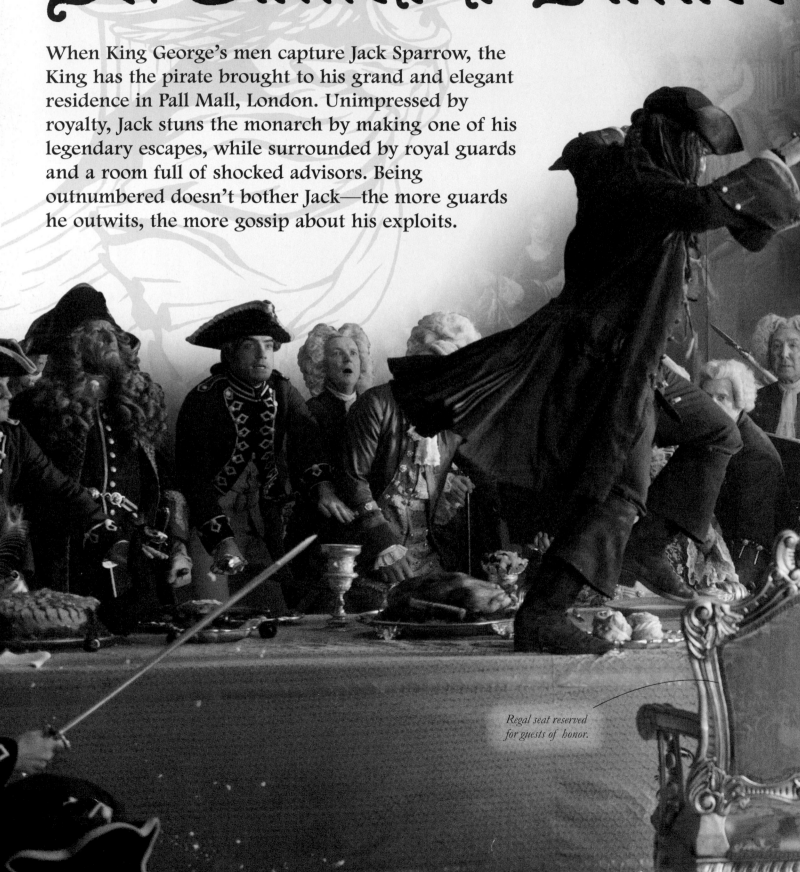

When King George's men capture Jack Sparrow, the King has the pirate brought to his grand and elegant residence in Pall Mall, London. Unimpressed by royalty, Jack stuns the monarch by making one of his legendary escapes, while surrounded by royal guards and a room full of shocked advisors. Being outnumbered doesn't bother Jack—the more guards he outwits, the more gossip about his exploits.

Regal seat reserved for guests of honor.

The Royal Guard haul Jack in for a special audience.

Feast for the Eyes

The royal banqueting table is always a feast for the eyes, but the King is more used to jellies in the shape of peacocks than the sight of a fleeing pirate. Jack is no stranger to high-flying antics with his experience of climbing ships' rigging, so he thinks nothing of swinging out of the room on a chandelier.

Red coat and gold braid denotes elite Royal Guard.

The scene of numerous bar room brawls.

Recruiting a Crew

A perilous voyage sounds a lot more tempting if it is proposed to you over a foaming ale, among merry companions in a cosy inn. This is the perfect place to assemble the desirable quantity of undesirables, with some cut-rate cutthroats thrown in for good measure.

Scuffed tables from the inn's patrons' knives and pistols.

The Captain's Daughter Inn

In the seedy wharf district of London, down by the reeking Thames, is a watering hole renowned for the roughness of its grog and the shadiness of its customers. No better place then to assemble a crew of sea dogs crazy enough to sail under the leadership of Captain Jack Sparrow…

The captain's daughter in the pub's sign wears a hat that suggests that the place is pirate-friendly.

Out of Tune

Countless sailors have attempted to impress the ladies with a tune and a ripping yarn after they have had too much liquor. Pub regular Scrum's tales stir hearts up to bravery that they may well regret.

High Spirits

You can't call it a good night at The Captain's Daughter unless there has been a fight or two. Many a score has been settled in the rafters of the back room, and this is where Jack is first united with his doppelgänger.

Angelica

She is the kind of woman who usually gets what she wants. But is this beautiful buccaneer after the Fountain of Youth or the heart of Jack Sparrow? Whatever Angelica's true aim, failure is not an option, as she has allied herself with the diabolical Blackbeard and a crew of the unquestioning undead.

Leather hat with pheasant plume.

Loose cambric shirt.

Mirror, Mirror...

They say imitation is the sincerest form of flattery, but old acquaintance Jack is far from delighted to discover he has a twin. Angelica proves she can match him in battle.

Angelic Charm

This cross necklace is a souvenir from Angelica's early years spent in a convent. Though those days are behind her, Angelica still keeps her faith strong and wears this necklace every day.

Plain cross of antique gold.

Crew Wanted

- To set sail for the Fountain of Youth by way of Whitecap Bay.

- To serve under the celebrated Captain Jack Sparrow.

- To enjoy the comradeship of diverse zombie shipmates.

- To ask no questions in order to be told no lies.

Angelica's beauty means that she can usually get whatever she wants.

Mystery Girl

Angelica returns into Jack's life to recruit him as Captain for Blackbeard's ship. But she has a mystery hanging over her head. Why would such a free spirit choose to serve one of the most formidable villains on the seas?

Sea of Heartache

Legend has it that Angelica is the only woman Jack Sparrow ever truly loved. Whether she broke his heart or he smote hers is the subject of endless debate between the two pirates. The truth could just be a matter of life and death.

Clam-shell design wristguard.

Telltale Blade

The worn leather and weathered studs on Angelica's swordbelt show that she is no stranger to dangers and duels on the high seas.

Second cross on gold bracelet for good measure.

The Secret of Eternal Youth

Throughout history, people have sought a way to remain young forever. This hope was regarded as just a dream, until the Spanish conquistador Ponce de León made his dramatic discovery. Now the British and Spanish know of the secret, the race is on...

Two Chalices

These cups, inscribed "Aqua" and "de Vida"—"water" and "of life"—have a worth beyond the silver from which they are fashioned. Stolen years ago from the city of Cartagena, the Chalices have seen many owners, and much blood has been spilled in their name.

The Profane Ritual

Legends tell that everlasting life can be found at the Fountain of Youth, but only those who possess the knowledge of the ancient ritual can achieve their heart's desire.

First, the two silver Chalices of Cartagena must be found, for the ceremony requires not just a seeker of youth but also a victim whose years will be consumed. Both must drink from the Chalices, at which point all the years of the victim's life will be transferred to the seeker.

A mermaid's tear may sound like one of the romantic ingredients of a quaint fairy tale, but in fact, no prize could be harder to win. As proud and ferocious as the sea they live in, mermaids do not weep lightly.

Whitecap Bay must then be reached, for only here can mermaids still be found. One of these beautiful yet savage creatures must be captured and forced to do the seeker's bidding. Only a mermaid's tear, placed in one of the Chalices, will set the rejuvenating forces to work.

Finally, the Fountain of Youth itself must be reached. Water will flow, with which the Chalices can be filled. The ceremony for immortality can now begin...

Agua de Vida

The Fountain of Youth

Through dense jungle, beyond the wreck of the *Santiago*, and past the Jungle Pools is this mystical spot where miracles are possible. Finding the Fountain is not enough, however—you need a guide who knows the right words to make the water rise up. Someone like Jack Sparrow.

Mao Kun Map

Prized above all other charts by treasure seekers, this map reveals, among other marvels, the location of the Fountain of Youth. Stolen from the Pirate Lord of Singapore, Sao Feng, it made its way to Jack Sparrow. Finally, it fell into the hands of Gibbs. With no fixed points, this chart is the only guide that takes into account the role of chance, fate, and the supernatural in mortal affairs.

Fantastic Voyage

In the right conditions, the central symbol on the map will depict the *Santiago*, and the map will show its owner the route taken by Ponce de León in 1523. Dates and distances can change, however, and mislead the traveler who uses the map unwisely.

AQUA DE VIDA

AQUA DE VIDA

Eternal Youth

To locate the prize of immortality, the map reader must line up the symbols correctly. The struggle for eternal life is symbolized by a tug of war between a skeleton and an angel. This must be aligned with the symbol of the Fountain of Youth—the Chalices.

地獄

Blackbeard

With a ravaged visage and a murderous glint in his cold eyes, Edward Teach is the most feared pirate of all. Known far and wide as Blackbeard, Teach is a ruthless killer and master of the dark arts. Now, a prophecy from his quartermaster says his time is up and his end foretold. Only the Fountain of Youth can help him win his greatest battle—with death itself.

Black Look

Dressed in leather as black as his own legendary deeds, Blackbeard strikes utter terror into lesser men with his mere presence.

The Legend

- Blackbeard got his name from his distinctive thick, dark beard.

- Blackbeard is known to keep the skeletons of his victims as trophies. He displays them in an unusual way...

His Edge

Brandishing the Sword of Triton, Blackbeard commands unearthly power. This weapon, which some say was forged in lost Atlantis, channels mystical power that brings dead matter to life.

Powder burns darken the barrel.

Rounded pommel doubles as a club.

Black leather grip.

Deadly Weapons

Blackbeard's formidable appearance is probably his best weapon, but he is always armed with his sword and at least one flintlock pistol.

Grooves strengthen and lighten blade.

Dark Thoughts

A dark philosophy inspires Blackbeard's diabolical actions. He feels closest to his Maker when he sees pain and suffering, and believes misery lifts the veil from reality, showing life as it truly is.

Broad steel handguard.

Saving Grace?

Known for his total lack of compassion, Blackbeard shows a rare concern for the fate of his supposed daughter Angelica. He claims he would give his soul to save her—a claim destined to be put to the test.

Every pirate captain flies his own variation on the Jolly Roger flag. Blackbeard's skull and flames reveals a passion for forbidden dark magic.

Whale-oil lanterns.

Crow's nest.

Stunning stained-glass window.

Queen Anne's Revenge

Bristling with cannons and spiked with human bones, the most feared ship on the seven seas belongs to the terrifying Blackbeard. Like a monstrous creature, the *Queen Anne's Revenge* comes to life—as long as its captain wields the Sword of Triton. Then the vessel will do his will, and spread terror in its bloody wake.

Sea Master

This fearsome frigate is heavily loaded with sails to keep it moving even in low winds. However, it also has a mysterious advantage over the other ships racing to the Fountain of Youth, holding no ordinary ship's crew but a terrifying mixture of pirates and zombies.

Torn sails.

Greek fire.

Bone Sweet Bone

Legends say that Blackbeard's ship was built by his victims. But take a closer look and you will see that it is actually constructed *from* them as well. Their skulls help to give the ship a tough outer shell.

Greek Tragedy

The secret weapon located in the bow of the *Revenge* is based on the Greek fire device of the ancient Byzantine Empire. Unleashed by a skeletal figurehead, a sulphurous spray spreads all the terrors of the inferno through enemy ranks.

Philip Swift

A captive, forced to join the crew of the *Queen Anne's Revenge* against his will, Philip Swift is a lonely voice of reason in a world of madness. The young missionary would have been slain long ago, but Angelica believes he holds the key to taming Blackbeard.

Leather-bound Bible with impression of cross.

Charmed Life

Philip's survival depends on Angelica. She fears for Blackbeard's soul if he kills Philip.

Thin leather cord.

Simple Faith

A man of few possessions, Philip needs little in life except for his cracked and weathered Bible and his simple cross necklace, which lies close to his heart.

Plain wooden cross.

Did you know?

Philip is lashed to the mast of the Queen Anne's Revenge. Despite this painful ordeal, the missionary still manages to cling onto his most precious effect—his holy Bible.

Key Facts

- Philip had been working as a missionary in the Caribbean.

- Blackbeard captured Philip during a raid on a remote island.

- According to the Pirate Code, Philip must die for refusing to serve Blackbeard.

- The missionary's task now is to save the blackest soul of all.

Deadly Truth

Fearlessly honest, Philip is the only man aboard the *Revenge* who dares call Blackbeard a coward. He thinks his captor is afraid to walk the path of righteousness. When Jack incites mutiny, Philip refuses to side with anyone. This puzzles the pirates: Can Philip do that?

Plain clothes reveal humble missionary lifestyle.

Swift Ending

Despite Angelica's pleas, Blackbeard orders the death of Philip. The zombie quartermaster is only too ready to spill mortal blood…

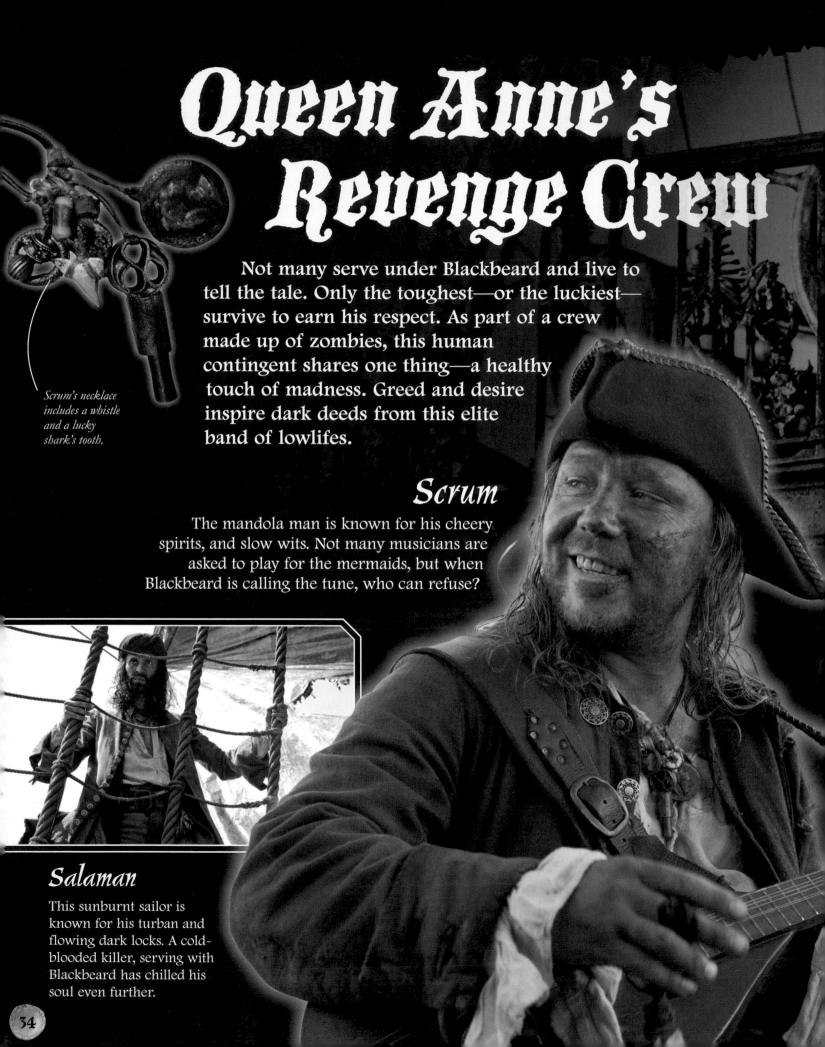

Queen Anne's Revenge Crew

Not many serve under Blackbeard and live to tell the tale. Only the toughest—or the luckiest—survive to earn his respect. As part of a crew made up of zombies, this human contingent shares one thing—a healthy touch of madness. Greed and desire inspire dark deeds from this elite band of lowlifes.

Scrum's necklace includes a whistle and a lucky shark's tooth.

Scrum

The mandola man is known for his cheery spirits, and slow wits. Not many musicians are asked to play for the mermaids, but when Blackbeard is calling the tune, who can refuse?

Salaman

This sunburnt sailor is known for his turban and flowing dark locks. A cold-blooded killer, serving with Blackbeard has chilled his soul even further.

SCRUM'S
SWORD

Cabin Boy

The cabin boy is a scrappy little survivor
whose toughness belies his diminutive size
—but it turns out that there is a touch of
the hero in this young pirate.

*Half-basket hilt
protects hand.*

*Scrum's mandola:
eight strings —all
out of tune.*

*Personal grooming at a
record low—even by
pirate standards.*

Ezekiel

They say time wears down the faces of
mountains, but old pirates just get craggier.
This weathered warrior has seen enough to
know that Blackbeard cannot escape the
fate predicted by his eyeless quartermaster.

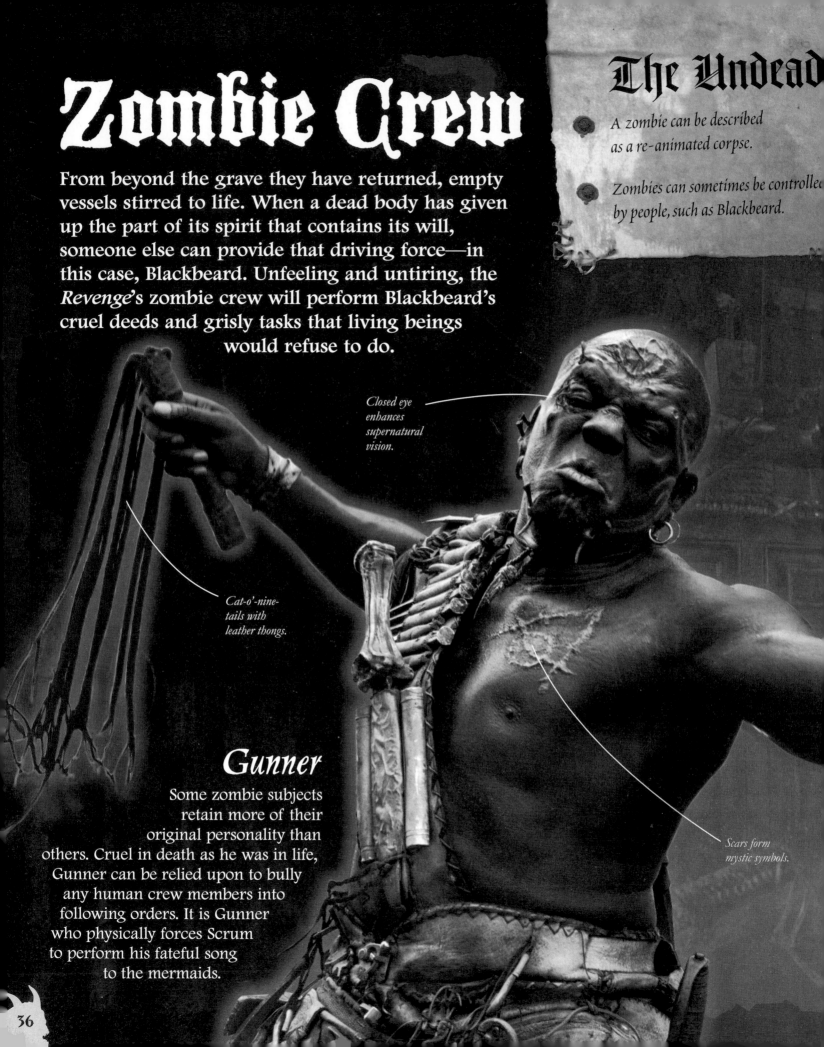

Zombie Crew

From beyond the grave they have returned, empty vessels stirred to life. When a dead body has given up the part of its spirit that contains its will, someone else can provide that driving force—in this case, Blackbeard. Unfeeling and untiring, the *Revenge*'s zombie crew will perform Blackbeard's cruel deeds and grisly tasks that living beings would refuse to do.

The Undead

- A zombie can be described as a re-animated corpse.

- Zombies can sometimes be controlled by people, such as Blackbeard.

Closed eye enhances supernatural vision.

Cat-o'-nine-tails with leather thongs.

Scars form mystic symbols.

Gunner

Some zombie subjects retain more of their original personality than others. Cruel in death as he was in life, Gunner can be relied upon to bully any human crew members into following orders. It is Gunner who physically forces Scrum to perform his fateful song to the mermaids.

Sew Scary

Sewn-up lips are one of the telltale signs that dark magic is at work. Some believe that the soul can escape the body through the mouth, so this precaution is taken to keep the spirit enslaved.

Beings of Burden

Devoid of feeling, efficient, and enduring like machines, zombies make ideal slaves for any form of tough physical labor.

Quartermaster

When dealing in the dark arts you can unleash powers beyond your control. Gifted with second sight, this undead quartermaster has foreseen Blackbeard's death.

Blackbeard's Inferno

The nightmarish vision painted on this
stained glass window depicts dead men
writhing in flames. The fires are being
stoked by devilish characters. The window
makes the cabin look truly fiendish.

Blackbeard's Cabin

It is said that Blackbeard is possessed of a tattered soul, lost to the forces of darkness. Just a glimpse into his private chamber confirms this suspicion. A space usually reserved for luxury, the captain's cabin on the *Queen Anne's Revenge* is more like the den of an evil magician. Dark dreams and schemes emanate from this murky lair.

Captain's Table

Blackbeard's inner sanctum is where he stows his potions and poisons, and all the paraphernalia of his dark arts. Lit by dripping candles and festooned with mystical artifacts, Edward Teach's lair is designed to fill any visitor with fear.

Dark Magic

Blackbeard is extremely fierce. All that aggression has resulted in a haggard face and dark-rimmed eyes.

Real human hair used on doll— sometimes taken from subject.

Born in the jungles of the Caribbean Isles, a sinister sorcery is spreading across the untamed regions of the world. Cunning men have learned how to harness the power of dark magic, but this magic is a double-edged sword, and can bring the downfall of the very ones who seek to use it.

Voodoo Victim

Blackbeard's box of magic tricks is full of surprises. Jack is shot with a dart dipped in a secret, sleep-inducing elixir to get him aboard the *Queen Anne's Revenge.*

Puppet Power

There are many ways to enslave unwilling victims through the dark arts, and one of Blackbeard's most trusted methods is the voodoo doll. Cruel actions performed upon the doll can be felt by the person it represents.

Buckle made from cloth, as metal can disrupt magic.

Real leather used for swordbelt.

Second Sight

Zombies may not have the eyesight of living men—but they can see things mortals cannot. Blackbeard's future has been foreseen by his quartermaster. Unless Blackbeard can cheat destiny itself, he will be killed by a pirate hunter with one leg.

Playing with Dolls

Blackbeard's voodoo doll also has an effect on Angelica, as Blackbeard's effigy of Jack allows Angelica to toy with Jack's emotions, too.

Family Issues

No one truly knows what cold calculations lurk in the mind of this seasoned buccaneer. Until the final game is played out it would be unwise to assume Blackbeard is a gullible fool, who really believes everything he is told. Is there a card yet to be played in this dangerous game of deception?

Cruel Choice

In order for Blackbeard to escape his inevitable death, he must steal fresh years at the Fountain of Youth. The question no one in his crew dares to ask is—from whom will he steal them?

Along with its counterpart, this beautiful Chalice has been the source of bitter treachery and bloodshed over the centuries.

Angelica and Blackbeard

Blackbeard and Angelica are a formidable partnership. Sharp-witted Angelica has a talent to dazzle and deceive, learned from Jack Sparrow himself, whereas Blackbeard is a master of the dark arts. But there is more to this collaboration than meets the eye: Some say Angelica is Blackbeard's daughter!

Devoted Daughter?

Blackbeard has been unbeatable since Angelica joined forces with him. She created the elaborate charade that ensured the capture of Captain Jack. She inspires loyalty in the living members of his crew and is becoming a notable apprentice. But Angelica wants Blackbeard to become a better man—and prevent his soul from descending into darkness.

Dark Deal

- *Angelica promises Blackbeard she will to get him to the Fountain of Youth and save his life.*

- *In return, Blackbeard gives Angelica the ship, crew, and supernatural resources to exact her revenge on Jack Sparrow.*

Providence

With its outsized Union Jack billowing in the breeze, this three~mast ship~of~war is the pride of the King's fleet. Built for battle, square~rigged for speed, and equipped for long tours of duty, there is no frigate better prepared to take on the ultimate quest—for the Fountain of Youth.

Deep Waters

A fair name doesn't guarantee a golden destiny. This vessel is heading for the mysterious Whitecap Bay, and there fate will truly show whether providence is on the side of its crew.

The crow's nest affords a view of the horizon twice as far as can be glimpsed on deck.

Furled jib on the bowsprit.

Did you know?

Hector Barbossa was previously captain of the Black Pearl, a ship that he took from Jack Sparrow under circumstances that can only be described as mutiny.

Barbossa's Cabin

The seven-windowed Great Cabin affords Barbossa a stunning view of the seas. Barbossa's secret naval charts are safely stowed here.

Reformed Pirate

Can you teach an old sea dog new tricks? Hector Barbossa is an ex-pirate who has received a Royal Pardon. Now, the *Providence* is ruled with an iron fist—no rum, no smoking, and no uncouth songs.

Providence Crew

The finest officers the Admiralty can produce team up with the best-drilled crew to provide the most formidable task force His Majesty can assemble. Under the command of Hector Barbossa, this worthy vessel sails forth on its quest without fear. Perhaps the crew would feel differently if they knew of some of the previous disasters its captain had taken part in…

HECTOR BARBOSSA

LIEUTENANT GROVES

Key Facts

- The *Providence* is a privateer, acting under letters of marque from the King.

- The crew can take any action, except fire upon nations with which Britain is not at war.

- They can only hope the crews of the three Spanish galleons they meet feel the same.

ILLETTE

Dream Team

Bewigged and resplendent in their new uniforms, Barbossa's officers Groves and Gillette are always ready to give him expert advice— which he ignores. The ex-pirate knows that Captain Jack's old first mate, Joshamee Gibbs, is the only one who truly understands the outlandish perils ahead.

JOSHAMEE GIBBS

Naval Files

The secret files of British Prime Minister Henry Pelham reveal his analysis of the strengths and weaknesses of his own force—and its pirate foe—as it races toward the Fountain of Youth. The *Providence* has the advantage on paper, but there are supernatural factors to be taken into account when it comes to Blackbeard's frigate.

Blackbeard

Operates in the West Indies. A clever strategist who employs fear as his weapon. Ruthless if driven to use force.

103 feet (31 meters)

Queen Anne's Revenge

FULLY RIGGED BATTLESHIP

Performance

Propulsion: Sails, 6,000 square yards (5,017 square meters).

Weapons: Greek fire, estimated 70 cannon.

Max. speed: Unknown. Claims of 20 knots under dark magic sail.

Displacement: 3527 tons (3,200 tonnes)

Crew: Approx. 200.

Admiralty analysis: The *Revenge* is light on crew numbers, but our observers suspect a 40 percent Zombie complement. Zombies are difficult to kill, as they are already dead.

Special intelligence: Location of Fountain of Youth known to a crew member.

H.M.S. Providence

SQUARE-RIGGED BARQUE

107 feet (32 meters)

Performance

Propulsion: Sails, 6,400 square yards (5,852 square meters).

Weapons: 80 cannon.

Max. speed: 9 knots.

Displacement: 3306 tons (3,000 tonnes)

Crew: Approx. 650.

Admiralty analysis: The *Providence* is the best vessel in the British fleet. The Navy's strongest officers are aboard. It is nigh unbeatable.

Special intelligence: Location of Fountain of Youth known to pirate held onboard—one Joshamee Gibbs.

Barbossa

Reformed pirate, previously captain of the Black Pearl. *Scourge of the Caribbean. Combines experience with almost reckless daring.*

AQUA DE VIDA

Jack and Angelica

They say all's fair in love and war, and there's little difference between those two extremes in the affairs of Jack and Angelica. A turning, twisting fate has bound them together for a second time, and they feel a mutual attraction, despite being a danger to each other. Now, Jack finds himself in the unusual position of trying to do the right thing—to help the damsel he may have once led astray.

Sailing Solo

Jack and Angelica may be made for each other, but Jack is a man who prefers his own, rather eccentric, company. After all, there is only one Jack Sparrow, despite Angelica's previous attempts to prove otherwise!

Deadly Dance

The passionate pair confesses their inner feelings as they dance on the deck of the *Queen Anne's Revenge*. Angelica admits she is drawn to Jack because he is untameable. Jack confesses that he thinks she smells nice.

Ring of Thieves

Jack gave this amethyst ring to Angelica during their first romance. In later years, she traded it with sorcerer Tia Dalma for the secret of the Profane Ritual. Jack spotted the ring in Tia's shack and promptly stole it back—returning it to Angelica once again during their second acquaintance.

Power Couple

In rare moments when Jack and Angelica are not pointing weapons at each other, they work together to find the Fountain of Youth. Jack knows where it is; Angelica knows how to perform the ritual when they get there.

The Mutiny

It is a dirty word to anyone who has ever captained a ship, but for once, Jack is prepared to utter it: Mutiny! Trapped on a ship crewed by zombies, going to a place of almost certain death, rebellion seems Jack's only option. However, his revolt is quickly stopped in its tracks when the sinister ship springs to life.

Rum Rebel

Jack uses his lowly position as mere crewman to rustle up support in every quarter. A persuasive tongue soon brings him enough men to achieve success—against any normal adversary.

Teach's Lesson

Resistance crumbles when Blackbeard arrives on deck. His dark magic is so powerful that even his ship follows his every demand, and it soon has Blackbeard's mutinous crew caught in its rigging. Blackbeard is pulling the strings once again, and the mutiny is doomed.

New Outlook

Ensnared by the ship's ropes, Jack is left to consider his future from a different angle. The ship's cook is blamed for the mutiny and is forced to return to work—as a zombie!

Whitecap Bay

The remote lighthouse at Whitecap Bay is of ancient design, with a convex lens standing in front of an oil-fired beacon. This beacon doubles as a harbor light.

Doom awaits any misguided mariner who seeks out the perilous waters of Whitecap Bay. Myths tell of mermaids lurking beneath the pale, foaming breakers, but few know that these briny beauties are actually flesh~eating creatures. When Blackbeard locates these denizens of the deep, he and his crew find themselves surrounded by vengeful foes consumed with rage against mankind.

No Escape

The cove's rocks offer no refuge from mermaids. They can survive long enough on land to drag a human back into the sea where they can entangle their foe in a powerful grip.

Gone Fishing

Blackbeard has hatched a plan to catch a mermaid, but he will not be doing the fishing himself. He has handpicked members of his crew for the dangerous job; the ones he can do without.

Hot Waters

A longboat full of members of Blackbeard's crew has a mission to lure a mermaid for her tears. Legend has it that man-made light and song attract the sirens of the sea, so the boat is lit by the beam of the lighthouse and Scrum sings a swaying sea shanty. Soon, the brittle boat is surrounded by more mermaids than its crew bargained for.

Prize Catch

Blackbeard's strategy has paid off: A fierce battle between the mermaids and his crew produces the prize he seeks. The pirates have caught a live mermaid, but at the cost of many of the crewmembers' lives. It is Philip Swift who strikes the wounding blow—an act he will come to regret.

Beautiful Creatures

A mermaid's radiant appearance is her greatest weapon. The light of the moon illuminates her skin, her long locks tumble seductively, and her deep-as-the-ocean eyes possess the power to entrap any adventurer.

The Mermaids

Sailors have speculated for centuries about these magical creatures. Half woman, half fish, they rise up from the waves to lure men into their arms. Captain Jack knows the terrible truth. He has always got along well with mermaids, but he knows that many ships' crews have met a terrible end at their hands.

Did you know?

When under the waves, the mermaids transform into very different creatures. They may look lovely, but they can shred a human limb from limb in seconds.

Kiss of Death

Scrum is almost powerless to resist a kiss from a beautiful mermaid, but succumbing to her otherworldly charms will lead to certain death.

Syrena

Hauled from her natural element, mermaid Syrena is a tormented creature, alone in a world of mortals and at the mercy of a dreaded captor. Yet she is not cruel like many of her kind, and her humanity calls out to a fellow spirit—one who could become her savior…

Land Maid

On land, Syrena loses her scaly aquatic form and assumes a gentle human shape. Unused to walking on two feet, and wounded, she is a stumbling, vulnerable figure— truly a fish out of water.

Mercy Mission

Philip Swift regrets capturing Syrena at Whitecap Bay. To make the pirates see her as a person and not a creature, he gives her the name of Syrena. He is the only human to treat her with any dignity.

Mermaid Tank

The pirates fashion a water tank to carry Syrena in. After all, mermaid tears don't keep; they must be harvested fresh.

Mermaid Death

Philip and Syrena discover a kindred connection and, with it, true love. But their newfound love may be short-lived, as Blackbeard is prepared to sacrifice them both in order to make his plan work…

The Santiago

Aboard the Santiago are the two chalices that are a crucial part of the ritual to gain eternal life.

AQUA DE VIDA

There are many myths of the seven seas, but the fate of few ships has been debated like that of the *Santiago*. Sent to discover the marvels of the New World in the sixteenth century, the ship has been missing ever since. Legends say that its captain, Ponce de León, discovered the Fountain of Youth. Now, the *Santiago* once again figures in the schemes of ruthless men.

Grisly Interior

Its rotting timbers exposed to the sun and wind, the *Santiago* is now a dank, insect-ridden ruin where creepers and cobwebs intertwine with discarded weapons and bleached human bones. Resplendent treasures lie in wait for anyone brave enough to set foot in this shadowy wreck.

Jack's Discovery

Perilously poised atop bare crags amid rushing waters, the long-lost *Santiago* is a vision to inspire awe in any heart. Stranded inland by an ancient storm, the vessel gently rocks on the edge of its own destruction.

Key Facts

- The *Santiago* lies hidden away in unchartered lands.

- No one knows whether the ship's commander, Ponce de León, ever truly went on to find the Fountain of Youth.

- Jack has made it this far before—but he never made it up to the wreck itself.

The Jungle Pools

Haunted by the cruel deeds that have occurred here over the centuries, the Jungle Pools are a mournful place, where the half~heard wailing of long~dead mermaids seems to linger in the air. Over the years, the waters have been used to trap mermaids in their marine form, while their captors endeavor to harvest their precious tears. Twisted skeletons among the pools reveal the many pitiless murders already committed here. The pools are connected by tunnels that could provide a way out for Syrena.

Marine skeleton and dead scales show body was left partly in the pools.

Fearful Journey

Under Blackbeard's orders, the crew takes Syrena to the dreaded Jungle Pools to harvest her precious tears. Meanwhile, Jack is at Ponce de León's ship, the *Santiago*.

Ray of Hope

Philip and Syrena's relationship seems destined to a grim end. Syrena, however, understands tragedy. The mermaid people believe that "the One pours death into life, and life into death, without a drop spilt."

Skeleton still bound to stake by wrists.

Remains of rope and hair reveal mermaid's death was in recent times.

Killing Time

Tying mermaids within reach of water, yet leaving their bodies to slowly dry out, is a cruel torture often seen at the pools. When the creatures die, they leave behind the remains of their marine form.

Reunion at Palm Tree Grove

These two old rivals discover they have a lot in common when they are forced to spend some quality time together again at the Spanish camp. Barbossa and Jack both have an enemy in Blackbeard, and both seek the Fountain of Youth—although for their own particular reasons. However, it could finally be time for the two ex-Captains of the *Black Pearl* to join forces.

Spanish Camp

Jack has his eyes on the prize when he and Barbossa infiltrate the enemy camp. The Chalices make a great bargaining tool when it comes to dealing with Blackbeard.

Hidden Resources

Jack looks on as Hector reveals there is more to Hector's wooden leg than meets the eye—it contains a hidden supply of rum and a handy cup. Jack is unfazed by this revelation—he saw through Barbossa's phony new image a long time ago. He is keen to share the rum, though.

Swinging Escape

Jack's dazzling escape—swinging from the palm trees—produces an unexpected bonus. The rain of coconuts knocks out several of the guards, and the resulting ballyhoo is taken by Barbossa's men to be the sign to attack. Jack even manages to circle one of the trees and tie some very bewildered Spaniards up in the progress. Now, *that's* improvisation!

The Ritual Begins

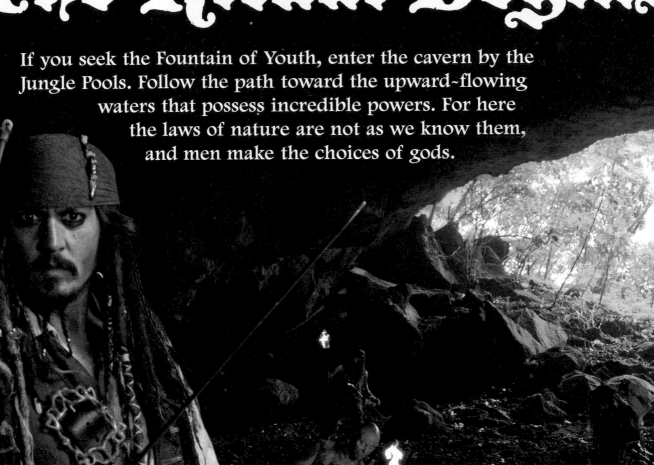

If you seek the Fountain of Youth, enter the cavern by the Jungle Pools. Follow the path toward the upward-flowing waters that possess incredible powers. For here the laws of nature are not as we know them, and men make the choices of gods.

Magic Words

Jack discovers that to enter the fountain's chamber he must speak the words inscribed upon the two Chalices: "Aqua de Vida."

Anyone daring enough to reach this remote spot would be wasting their time without these vessels.

Enchanted Waters

This is it—the sacred chamber men have sought for centuries. Exotic creepers and clinging moss cover ancient skeletons that litter the stone steps, and a delicate stream of enchanted water flows through a natural stone circle.

The Final Step

Blackbeard's ragged band stumbles wearily to its destination. It is too late to turn back. Here, at the end of their quest, the surviving members of the crew know the sacrifice the ritual requires. At least one of them will not be walking out.

Judgment Day

Some men are beyond redemption, it is said—even given the place, the time, and the power to make up for all their wickedness. At this place of miracles, will Edward Teach prove that his soul can be saved?

Stranger Tides

A lonely beach and a stranded mariner—it's a familiar scenario to Captain Jack. Except this time, he's doing the marooning. He believes the only fitting tribute he can pay to the great love that he and Angelica share… is to leave her. He has paid his debt to her and is now a free man—or so he thinks. As one adventure ends, the far-off horizon beckons with promises of new treasures to be had. Jack certainly has one precious gem in mind: Will he ever again be the captain of a certain *Black Pearl*?

Index

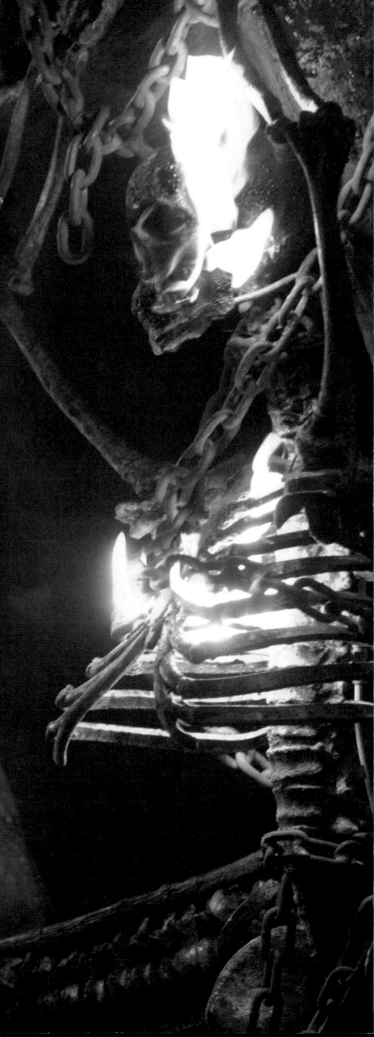

LONDON, NEW YORK, MELBOURNE,
MUNICH, AND DELHI

Project Editor Victoria Taylor   Publishing Manager Catherine Saunders
Editor Hannah Dolan   Art Director Lisa Lanzarini
Senior Designer Lynne Moulding   Associate Publisher Simon Beecroft
Designers Nick Avery, Rhys Thomas,   Category Publisher Alex Allan
Toby Truphet   Production Editor Clare McLean
Managing Art Editor Ron Stobbart   Production Controller Nick Seston

First published in the United States in 2011
by DK Publishing
375 Hudson Street, New York, New York 10014

10 9 8 7 6 5 4 3 2 1
002—180059—Feb/11

DK books are available at special discounts when purchased in bulk for sales
promotions, premiums, fund-raising, or educational use.
For details, contact: DK Publishing Special Markets,
375 Hudson Street, New York, New York 10014. SpecialSales@dk.com

A catalog record for this book is available from the Library of Congress.

ISBN: 978-0-7566-7219-5

Color reproduction by Alta Image, UK
Printed and bound by Lake Book Manufacturing Inc., U.S.A.

The publisher would like to thank Laura Gilbert for her editorial assistance
and Chelsea Alon, Dale Kennedy, Erik Schmudde, and Shiho Tilley at
Disney Publishing.

Discover more at
www.dk.com